To Wendy Anderson Halperin,
for her beautiful pictures,
with love!
—J. A.

To Jim Aylesworth, Ann Bobco, and Mr. Swagerty's smile
—W. A. H.

Atheneum Books
for Young Readers
An imprint of Simon & Schuster Children's
Publishing Division
1230 Avenue of the Americas
New York, New York 10020

Book design by Ann Bobco

The text of this book is set in Goudy Oldstyle BT.
The illustrations are rendered in colored pencil.

Manufactured in China

14 16 18 20 19 17 15

Library of Congress Cataloging-in-Publication Data
Aylesworth, Jim.
The full belly bowl / by Jim Aylesworth ; illustrated by Wendy anderson Halperin.—1st ed.
p.   cm.
Summary: In return for the kindness he showed a wee small man, a very old man
is given a magical bowl that causes problems when it is not used properly.
ISBN 0-689-81033-4 (ISBN-13: 978-0-689-81033-6) (alk. paper)
[1. Fairy tales.] I. Halperin, Wendy Anderson, ill. II. Title.
PZ8.A95Fu   1998   [E]—dc21   98-14052

0316 SCP

THE FULL BELLY BOWL

JIM AYLESWORTH

illustrated by

WENDY ANDERSON HALPERIN

ATHENEUM BOOKS FOR YOUNG READERS

In a tiny house at the edge of a forest, there once lived a very old man and a cat.

The cat, whose name was Angelina, was white with patches of black, and the very old man thought that she was just about the sweetest cat in the whole world.

On the day that this story begins, the very old man, hungry as usual, left Angelina on the sunny doorstep and went off into the forest in search of wild strawberries.

He had not gone far when he heard
the sound of a small voice
in great distress . . .

At once, the very old man picked
up a stick and ran toward the voice.
In a small thicket of trees, he
found that a fox had taken hold

of a wee small man and was
trying to carry him away.
"Stop!" shouted the
very old man,

"Let me go!"
yelled the voice.
"Let me go!"

and he threw the stick, hitting the fox
on the rump. Startled, the fox dropped
his prey and ran off into the brush.

The very old man could see that the wee small man was injured and needed some help. So he gently lifted him into his arms and carried him home.

Once there, he bandaged the wee small man's leg and set about making him comfortable. He was curious, of course, about the wee small man and where he came from, but he was too polite to ask, and the wee small man didn't say.

Nevertheless, for the next three days, the very old man extended his guest every courtesy, and shared generously from his meager pantry. He even mended the wee small man's torn vest.

Each day the wee small man grew stronger, and the two of them got along very well. Then, on the morning of the fourth day, the wee small man was gone without a word.

A few days later, the very old man found a letter on the doorstep. It was held beneath the rim of an overturned bowl.

The letter was so small that the very old man had to hold it with his fingertips.

Dear Friend,

In appreciation of your kindness and generosity,
I leave you this Full Belly Bowl.
You need never know hunger again.
Use it wisely or it will be a burden.
To empty, pour it out.
When not in use, store it upside down and
out of reach of children.

The letter wasn't signed.

Clearly the bowl
was a gift from the wee
small man, wherever he was, and
it was intended to be used for food.
Around the top of the bowl, there were
words written in a language that the very old
man had never seen.

"What on earth is a
Full Belly Bowl?" wondered
the very old man as he sat at the
table with his cat, Angelina. It was larger
than the other bowls he owned, and prettier,
too, with decorations of flowers and mysterious
birds.

So that evening, the very old man prepared a stew and poured it into the Full Belly Bowl.

As usual, he began to eat. Yet, after eating and eating and eating, the bowl was still as full as when he began. He ate and ate and ate some more, and still there was no change. Finally, he poured the stew out into another bowl for Angelina.

At last, the Full Belly Bowl was empty.

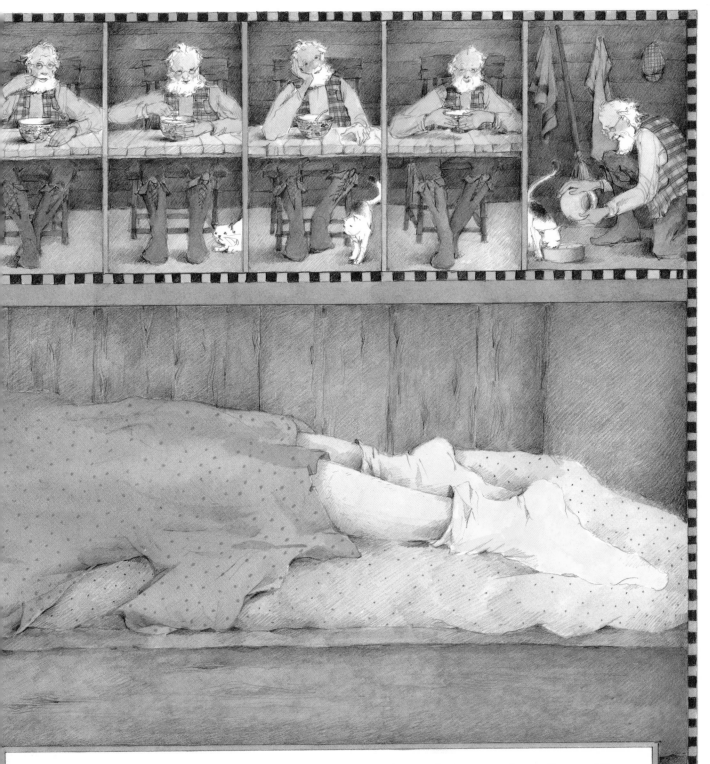

But the very old man certainly wasn't, and neither was Angelina. She was used to catching mice for her dinner and had never had more than a scrap or two from the table in her entire life.

Both had to lie down, and when they did, they fell asleep.

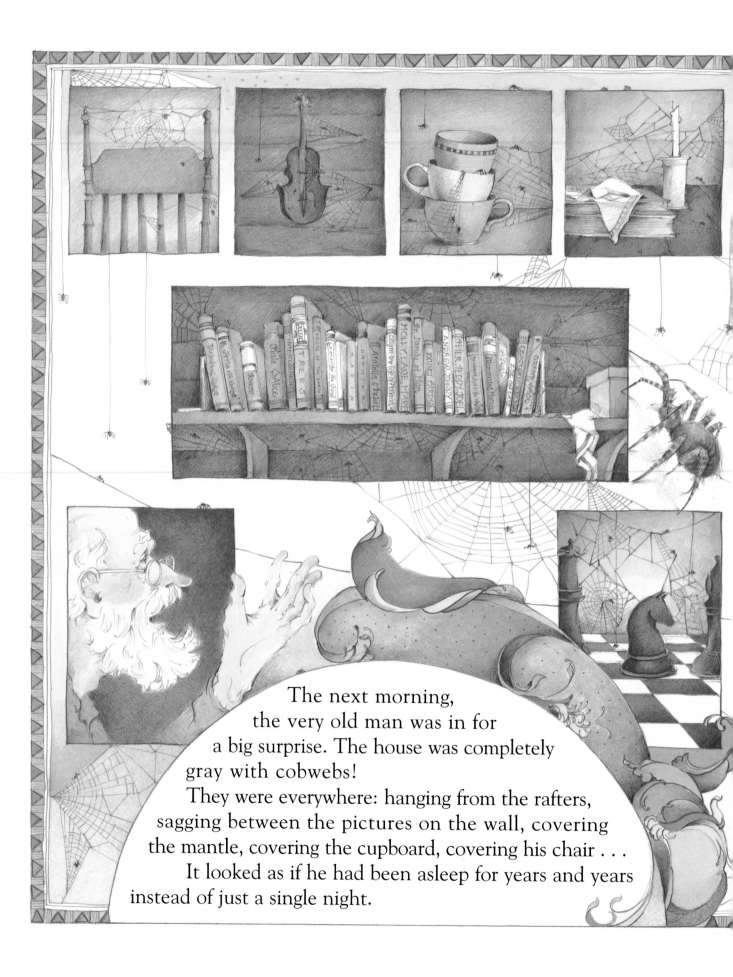

The next morning,
the very old man was in for
a big surprise. The house was completely
gray with cobwebs!
They were everywhere: hanging from the rafters,
sagging between the pictures on the wall, covering
the mantle, covering the cupboard, covering his chair . . .
It looked as if he had been asleep for years and years
instead of just a single night.

Then he saw the spiders!
One after the other, they were
streaming out of the Full Belly Bowl.

So it works with other things! thought the very old
man. Quickly, he turned the bowl over, and the parade
of spiders stopped.

The very old man spent the next weeks ridding the house of spiders and getting used to using the Full Belly Bowl properly. He made many delightful discoveries. He found, for instance, that he could multiply a single strawberry by placing it in the bowl and then repeatedly removing the strawberries until he had a heaping mound, all plump and sweet. When he had enough, he poured the last one onto the pile and put the bowl away.

Indeed, the
very old man
soon forgot the meaning of hunger.
In fact, he began to put on a little weight,
and, what with all the extra food being given
to her, so did Angelina. The very old man
didn't forget the spider problem, however,
and when he wasn't using the bowl, he
turned it upside down and put it on the top
shelf in the pantry.

Then one morning, he made another exciting discovery.
He had finished breakfast and was returning the bowl to the pantry when a button popped off his vest. It landed in the Full Belly Bowl. When he reached in and took it out, it was immediately replaced by another one in the same way that the spiders and the strawberries were.

It made him wonder what would happen if he put a coin in the bowl, and though the only coin he had was a copper penny, he decided to give it a try.

To his delight, it worked! Each time he took a coin from the bowl, he found that another had taken its place.

The very old man spent the rest of the morning taking pennies from
the bowl. He worked until his arm ached and the piles of pennies began
to spill off onto the floor.

It was then he realized that if he had a gold coin, he could put that into the bowl and, with the same small effort, make himself rich beyond his dreams!

He decided to take the pennies to town and swap them for gold. His hands trembled with excitement as he swept the pennies off the table and into an old flour sack.

With the heavy sack slung over his shoulder, he closed the door behind him and, leaving Angelina napping on the doorstep, he set off for town.

Unfortunately, the very old man had been so excited at the thought of becoming rich that he had forgotten to put the bowl away.

And even worse, in the days before the bowl, Angelina had kept the house free of mice, but now, with so much other food around, she

hadn't taken as much interest in them. And worst of all, one of the mice, a great big one, thought he smelled something good to eat in the Full Belly Bowl and started climbing up the very old man's chair, which was right next to the table.

While that mouse
was climbing up his chair,
the very old man was
swapping his pennies for three
ten-dollar gold pieces.
Right away, he put one of them in
his pocket to save for the Full
Belly Bowl.

Village Inn

Village Inn Rooms

With another, he bought
a pair of new boots and a fancy
new vest with brass buttons. And
since it was getting late, and he was
worn out from lugging that heavy sack
of pennies, he decided to spend the third
coin on a splendid dinner and a night's
lodging in a comfortable hotel.

By noon the next day, the very old man was home again. And one look at Angelina, with her nose pressed against the bottom of the door and her tail twitching, was enough to tell him that there was something wrong inside.

And sure enough, there was!
. . . Mice!
. . . Everywhere!
. . . Great big ones!
As fast as he could, the very old man made his way over to the table and dumped the last mouse out of the Full Belly Bowl. Then he stood looking at Angelina.

She was chasing around in a frenzy, doing her best, but not knowing which mouse to go after first.

Thinking fast, the very old man picked her up, gently folded her legs, and set her down in the Full Belly Bowl.

As soon as he took his hands away, Angelina jumped out again. And just that fast, she was replaced by another cat that looked exactly like her. That cat jumped out to be replaced by a third, and so on until the house was wild with black-and-white cats chasing hundreds of mice.

Very likely, those cats would still be jumping out of that Full Belly Bowl to this day if one of them hadn't chased a mouse up onto the table and knocked the bowl onto the floor.

It shattered to pieces!

Still, the cats kept chasing after the mice, and by evening, there wasn't a single mouse left in sight.

Though relieved to be rid of the mice, the very old man was sad at first that the Full Belly Bowl was broken. It had been nice not being so hungry all the time.

But it had caused a lot of trouble, too — and except for all of the cats, life soon returned pretty much to normal.

He never saw the wee small man again, and he never got another Full Belly Bowl.

He did keep that ten-dollar gold piece, however, and he promised himself that he would be much more careful next time, if there ever was a next time.

And because they never sat still long enough to be counted, he never found out how many cats there were, and he never found out which one was Angelina.

But in the end, it really didn't matter much.

The truth is, he loved them all. To him, they were just about the sweetest cats in the whole world!